DEER ME!

WRITTEN BY:

J. HOLLY McCAIN

May "Dear Me" be
as dear to you as it
is to me!
J. Holly M.

Palmetto Publishing Group, LLC
Charleston, SC

For more information regarding special discounts for bulk purchases, please contact Palmetto Publishing Group at Info@PalmettoPublishingGroup.com.

ISBN-13: 978-1-944313-75-3
ISBN-10: 1-944313-75-3

I dedicate this book to God, Jesus and The Holy Spirit. I would not have the gift of words without the blessing from my Amazing Father! I know Dear Lord; you will guide my thoughts for my next book.

Acknowledgements

First, I would like to thank those we have lost since I started writing my book. I thank my pup, Shadow. Shadow was always there to show me Gods world through her beautiful, brown eyes. Sasha, our sweet kitty cat, was always in a hiding spot, to dash out with her finds. Sasha, even though I didn't love the mouse you presented me, thank you for being my friend. I'm sorry you got lost in our new house and not given the attention you deserved. We did love you! To Virgil, thank you for all the memories. I will cherish each and every one of them. My sweet niece, Lily, I know we will meet in Heaven when I go home. Last, but not least, I bless the memories of my dear friend, Crystal.

Second, I would like to express gratitude to my family Shirley, Beth, Larry, Kylee, Cole, Emma, Faith, Tom, Tabie, John, Jacob, Sadie, Sassie, Dave and my other siblings; for always supporting, encouraging me. Big thanks to Shirley for posing for me, and biting the apple. I know how you hate having your picture taken. Hugs! Thank you for not discouraging me when my dream seemed so far away. I know all will be beside me through the next chapter of my life.

I'm grateful, for Reverends Nariah Edwards, Mac Kelly and Jim McClaren; without your sermons, I would not be where I am today in my spiritual discovery. And thank you Diane Linch and the children in the children's room at Fields United Methodist Church North Ridgeville, Ohio. Your critics on my work were appreciated. I'm sorry it took so long to publish my work.

My dear friends, Betty, John and Annette who bought every book and newspaper I was in. I thank all three of you for your encouragement. I thank Crystal's son Treyvon. Your mom loved my books, and encouraged me. Westerly Elementary School Bay Village, Ohio, and all schools whom let me read my two Puppy Poetry books in your schools. Thank you for your love of reading.

And finally, my heartfelt thank you to my city for its beautiful parks, and Jenny's Popcorn. You helped me make my book a fun to write about. Huge thanks to Lagoon Deer Park in Sandusky, Ohio. We loved feeding the animals, blessings for 58+ more years in business. My friends, loyal readers, fellow writers, I thank all of you for the last 16 years. Without, all of you, I would not have anyone to write for or about. I would like to thank 95.5 The Fish, my dear radio station; your personalities and blessed music has comforted me during my trying times of editing. Prayers my work helps many know God is always here, just call His name. Blessings!

TABLE OF CONTENTS

Chapter One
Welcome to Westerly

My name's Jules Currier. I guess you'd call me a dreamer, because whenever I get bored, my mind wanders all over the place. I know this, but that's not the reason for all the fuss in Westerly. But I'm getting ahead of my story. Let me first tell you about my city, Westerly, Ohio.

Westerly, Ohio is a small but quaint city in the eastern corner of Latrain County. It's about 18 miles southwest of the big city of Trey, Ohio, yet we're a stone throw away from their county line, go figure!

There are around 22,338 people in our community. A good portion of the adults have jobs in Kyle County, the county Trey is in. We have three elementary schools, one junior high and a high school. We also have a few parks. One named North Center. North Center is a beautiful park, but I guess I could be telling you this because it's my park. It has a nice path, circling a fishing pond. When you come to our city you can check it out yourself, please be careful of the duck and goose poop. They just can't seem to help themselves!

The folks of Westerly pride in not only being the 'Festival Capital' of the county but being darn good folks too. We not only have a great Popcorn Festival to celebrate each year with fireworks the first night, but we can throw a pretty good Fourth of July firework celebration too! The whole city, well not everyone, I'm just getting carried away with the excitement of telling you my story, but many, come out early to get a good seat. The fireworks start around 10:00pm, and you can see folks carrying chairs to North Center Park around 6:00 or 7:00pm! There are even people that sell food like hotdogs and of course, popcorn! Yes, fireworks are a really important thing in our city. I guess that's why they start asking for donations around July 5th, the day after the Fourth of July celebration every year!

My friend, Ann told me that that the smoke from fireworks is mostly dust. Did you know that? The smoke can have sulfur-coal mixed and maybe even gases in it! I myself wonder what happens in the sky after they're set off. Ann says the fire department puts them off because of fires. I guess that's why they set the fireworks off at the park because of the fish pond.

They do this so there won't be a fire. Do you think so too? Yes, I always wonder about fireworks and what happens from them, but I'll tell you more of our story in a little while, ok?

The Mayor of our city, Larry McClaren, can be seen at Lent fish fries, Sunday church and sometimes even the local grocery store. I guess even the Mayor of Westerly needs to eat and worship, what do you think?

We have two Pastors in our Congregation, well the Church the Mayor and I happen to go to. The first Pastor is Pastor Lily Linch. Pastor Linch reminds me of a butterfly. A butterfly flies flower to flower sipping its nectar to pollinate the plants. Pastor Linch takes her beautiful messages of the good book; you know the Bible, and delivers wherever she goes!

The second pastor is Pastor Lucas Allen. I don't know who's full of more stories, the Pastor or me. He's from the southern part of our state. He uses his down home stories a lot of times to teach us the Bible! He told us one once about the time his father taught him to climb on his horse. He told him to take an egg and crack it over the horse's head, and being dumb, the horse would be thinking about that egg on his head not the person mounting him. Well, a few cartons of eggs later, he still wasn't galloping in the field but wondering how to explain to mom why he wasted a weeks' worth of eggs! So, who was the dumbest that day! The sermon that followed, well after the congregation stopped laughing that is, *"Do not judge, or you too will be judged."* I bet the horse would've loved that sermon! What do you think?

We have many animals in our city. I've heard some stranger call us a 'Hick Town,' but what'd he know? Like the good book says, *"Do not judge, or you too will be judged. For in the same way you judge others, you will be judged, and with the measure you use, it will be measured back to you."* Did you know that comes from the Bible book of Mathew 7: 1-5? And Pastors Linch and Allen both wonder if I'm listening in church! But, let's get back to my story. When you drive through Westerly, you can see horses, cows, chicken, quail, and even alpaca's! One lady even raises skunk! Now, we won't comment on that will we?

There are friendly people in our city, take my friend, WB's parents, Michael and Wave Kordic. They live on Willow Tree Court. The Kordic's will give you the last pea on their plate, that's if you like peas! Ha! I do, don't you? Here I go getting away from the story again. Like I was telling you, these folk are one of the finest of Westerly. Do you know they haven't even been nominated Popcorn Couple of the year yet? Maybe they will be after this story! Mr. Kordic and Mrs. Kordic help other neighbors by shoveling driveways in the winter and mowing lawns in the summer. Good folks, the Kordic's!

Mr. Kordic, a bank president, loves to golf and take walks. You can see him walking down Willow Tree Court, and surrounding streets, in evenings. Don't look for him on Saturdays though, he likes to golf that day.

Mrs. Kordic owns our local pet food store, Wag-Your-Tail Barkery. Pets are allowed to go in to check-out the toys and treats. They make some real good dog treats in this store, if I have to say so myself! Hum! They have 'Halloween Pawties,' 'Weddings,' even an event called 'Barkstock,' in August of every year. Dogs with their human parents get to play games, enter contests and have a 'Barking good time'! I just love sitting back watching, the Pet look-alike contest. I'm telling you they shouldn't sell a pet to anyone that doesn't look like him or her. What do you think?

Mrs. Kordic bakes Puppy Pawty treats too! Cakes, ice cream, even hats are a few of the many items in her store. Hey, you can even have a Pawty in her store for your dog! You must come check this place out sometime. Just tell her Jules sent you, alright?

Next door to the Kordic family lives Mayor McClaren, his wife, Maria and their sons, Jacob and Austin. I consider Jacob my friend, but not many people like him. He 'walks around with his problems on his shoulder,' as my Grandma calls it. Jacob's bigger than the other 10 year olds. He's like the size of a Junior High School student and he's only in Elementary School! We like to play together and take walks in the field behind the school. We have a contest to see who spots the first deer. I always win 'because to me deer are great! I don't let him win, even when he's sad. Mom said that'd teach him just 'because he was sad, he'd win. And that'd be cheating, right? Jules Currier doesn't cheat! Jacob climbs trees and fishes better than I can. Our friendship's built on hanging out and doing stuff we both like.

Down the street from me on Rose Court, lives my good friend, Ann Ostrander. She's tall. I'm short. She can outstare me. She's a leader, where I'm sort of a follower. She loves to watch storms and doesn't mind being in them. I'm scared to death of lightening and would rather be in my basement then outside watching Mother Nature having one of her own fireworks displays, thank you! I think that's why we are such good friends. Where I'm weak, she's strong.

And where she's weak, I'm strong. So we make a great team. What do you think?

Ann has a dog named Sadie. Sadie and our dog, Shadow, are a couple. We never actually took them to get married on Valentine's Day at Wag-Your-Tail Barkery; we just know they were a couple. Did I tell you that I saw them kiss? They even exchange presents on Sweetest Day, Valentine's Day, and yes all the major holidays, or rather their "parents" do.

Sadie and Shadow love to play and take walks together. The problem sometimes one or both of them have their own idea of taking a walk. Sadie, well he's part Greyhound. He gets excited when he sees another dog or bike. It's like we're not going on a walk, but a triathlon! Sadie loves to show-off to Shadow. When Shadow and Sadie are together, Sadie almost always acts up. My Shadow, well she's shy and sometimes she just doesn't want to go for a walk. And when Shadow doesn't want to take a walk, she just stops right there, whether it's in the middle of the street or a driveway, and nothing or nobody can move her. Yes, those two, like Ann and I, are opposites in every way, but perfect for each other too! Ann and I spend the night at each other's house, many of weekends.

Next door to Ann lives the Appletree Family. Mr.

Appletree is the owner of Fields Homes. His company built our home. They will design and build many more in our growing development. His wife, Carol, is a real estate agent. They have two children, Dennis and Brenda. The Appletree children, much like their parents, think 'their poop doesn't stink.' Brenda doesn't appear to like me, nor I her. Dennis and Ann are arch enemies.

Dennis and Brenda keep teasing us about our hill. My friends and I meet at this hill almost every day. One day, the hill, which has almost become a friend to us, will be a house. The hill, if it could talk, could tell you many of our secrets. So, Brenda and Dennis tease us that this hill, so special to us, will be plowed down and made into a house by their father's company. What a bummer!

I guess it's about time I tell you about myself. You already know my name, Jules Currier. You know I'm a dreamer. Maybe someday I'll take this talent and become an actress or writer. Who knows, but I like being me. I love hanging out with my friends, writing, reading and photography. I enjoy taking nature shots. The zoo is one of my favorite spots. I just hate seeing the animals caged. What bothers me the most is when people knock on the glass window. Don't they understand it scares the animals? I don't photograph deer. I worry deer might think a camera is a gun and run. I take memory photos of them, storing their pictures in my mind forever.

I have one brother, Ed. Ed can come on as shy, but he's just getting to know you and checking you out at the same time. He's a very independent person. If Ed thinks he can do something, nothing or nobody is going to stop him, not even Westerly's whole police department! Yes, when my brother believes in something, he will get impatient with anyone or anything that gets in the way of reaching his goal.

Across the street from us, lives a couple by the name of Greg and Lorraine Henry. They have three cats. Mr. Henry may be one of the most cat loving guys I've ever met in my 12 years. I may meet another, who knows! He's just unique in his own way. Mrs. Henry already knows who her husband's first loves are! Yes, not another human, but those fur balls that purr and run the household! You might see Mr. Henry and his cat, Francois going to the mailbox some weekday around 4:30pm. Please just don't beep your horn when you see them. Sometimes loud sounds frighten a few of us people and hair balls.

Mrs. Henry, well she loves all nature. She can be seen working in her beautiful yard. Maybe you saw her put in that new walkway. Or plant the trees and bushes that are making a comforting surrounding for her to live in. She's planted some pretty flowers too. Yes, Mrs. Henry loves nature. People can be a problem, though. They just don't understand Mrs. Lorraine Henry, and to like Mrs. Henry is to know her. And to know her, you just got to give her a chance to get the feel of you as a person too. She's a solitary woman that Mrs. Henry. Yes, the Henry's pretty much stick to themselves, but you get out-of-line, like my friend, Katie Almost, and watch out!

Hey, let's stop laughing at Katie's name! The girl's been teased **ALMOST** all her ten years of life! Sorry, Katie, I just couldn't help the last sentence! Katie's dad, Mac Almost, was born in Canada, moving to Niagara Falls, New York in his early teens. Katie's mom is from Buffalo, New York. They met when Mr. Almost was stationed at Fort Drum, New York. Fort Drum is a training site for Army recruits, such as, Mac Almost. Mac and his buddies were having diner one evening at the little dinner Betty Shaw worked. They fell in love after Betty **ALMOST** spilled a cup of coffee on Mac Almost. Sorry, Katie, I just had to poke a little more 'fun' into the story. Well, they fell in love. When he finished serving time in the service, Mr. Almost went to the police academy. He works for the Westerly Police Department.

Katie, being both a "military brat," and police officer's child, won't give in. She likes to "get Lorraine Henry's goat," as my Grandpa Virgil calls it. Katie plays different tricks on Lorraine Henry. They may have what Grandpa Virgil calls a generation gap. I guess it's because one's about 60 and the other's 10. So, there's 50 years between them, like that's a lot! I know my Math teacher, Ms. San Jose would be so proud of me. She says people rely on calculators too much now.

Yes, that Friday morning, began as any old summer morning on our street. The songs from Kingfisher, geese, and crows could be heard. The blond mallard at the corner farm yodeled his good morning tune. Maybe an eagle could be seen in the August sky, or a beautiful butterfly floating. The sound of bike tires screeching, and skateboards sliding on the pavement, meant my friends, Katie, WB and the others were outside playing. The garage door at the Henry home was open. Lorraine Henry must be working in the yard.

"Wrrr..." the sound of her weed edger, much like fingernails on a chalkboard, filled my brain.

Where's Ann you ask? She's at a woodworking class. Yep, where I love writing, Ann loves working with wood. Don't get me wrong, I love the smell of fresh cut wood, but Jules Currier in a woodworking class? Nope! They don't have enough doctors in the emergency room at our local hospitals to care for me! I'm accident prone. Don't have anything sharp near Jules Currier. I cut myself just using scissors!

Ann and I would see each other later. My Mom would drive us to the Popcorn Festival in the evening. Mom said Ann and Sadie could also spend the night. We figured if Ann and I hung out, why shouldn't Shadow and Sadie too. Ann and I promised Pastor Allen we'd help at the church booth. Afterwards, we'd ride a few rides, play a few games and eat popcorn of course, supplied by our very own 'Popcorn Factory.' Yes, we also have a Popcorn Factory in our city. You can smell the popcorn a half a mile away! They make all different flavors, like chocolate, lime, strawberry, and my favorite, cherry popcorn. So, when you come to Westerly, Ohio, be sure to stop in and get some popcorn alright?

Why is corn so important to the people of Westerly, Ohio? The truth is...I don't know and I've lived in this city for 12 years! Now that I have you real confused maybe we can answer the question after we finish the first puzzle, what happened that August day in Westerly, OH?

Chapter Two
Trouble on Our Street

I ate an apple for breakfast that morning. I wanted to preserve a hungry appetite for tasting the new flavors of popcorn at the Popcorn Festival.

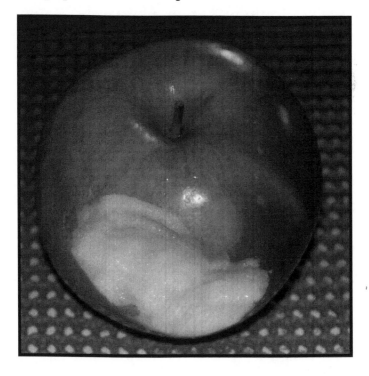

A few hours of chores would take my attention.

I glanced at Shadow. "Shadow, do you want to play for a while?" I asked out loud, "And then I'll do my chores. We could maybe play a little soccer." Shadow loves to chase the ball. She puts her little paw on it to claim it. Yes, Shadow doesn't ask for much, maybe a pet or walk once in a while. "So, do you want to play or walk, Girl?" Shadow answered that question. She carried me her leash. So, I guess my pal knew what she wanted, a walk. So, a walk it would be!

I could now see Mrs. Henry carrying her weed edger. She was dressed in her normal shorts, top and straw hat. The curtain in the Henry living room window moved. Hey don't get worried. It's only Francois, Sassie and Sasha. Francois, Sassie and Sasha are the Henry's three cats. I don't know who was more curious in Mrs. Henry, her cats, or WB and Katie. They like the cats were peeking at Mrs. Henry. No silly, they weren't in the house! The two kids were peeking around one of the Henry's bushes.

Yep, the cats were sure curious of their mom. Katie, well, she was just curious of what mischief she could do that day. Yes, cats and kids, ready to pounce on their next adventure! If you looked real close, maybe you caught Katie's sneer. I did! Or Mrs. Henry's stare. I caught that too. I never thought a little incidence like this would or could change a whole city, but this is Westerly, Ohio, so anything could happen!

"Hey!" yelled Mrs. Henry. "I thought I told you two to stay out of our yard!!!"

I'm sorry, if Mrs. Henry thought her roar would scare them, she was mistaken! I could see my two friends whispering to each other.

Shadow brought me my shoes. I guess the girl really wanted a walk. I put my shoes on and we started out our door for our adventure.

"My drive-way!" yelled Mrs. Henry. "It's a mess! Clean it up NOW!!" she snapped.

"Please, Mrs. Henry…!" I heard Katie reply, slapping the back of her neck. I know she was letting us know she thought Mrs. Henry was a "pain in the neck."

I groaned to myself. Yep, it was only ten minutes since I'd looked out the window. Now, ten minutes later, Mrs. Henry stood over Katie and WB. And Katie was doing our code for 'someone being a pain.' Prayers Mrs. Henry doesn't see.

Mrs. Henry's arms were raised up. I swear the lady looked like she was trying to chop something! Katie and WB waved right back! I couldn't hold back a laugh. Mrs. Henry, a straw hat on her head. Her body soaked from the sun. My two friends cleaning a mess-up they caused. An amusing site, though in reality not funny.

"If you think those fireworks tonight will be the only thing that explodes, kids, just wait until Greg gets home and sees what you did to his driveway!" Mrs. Henry threatened.

"Woof! Woof!" Shadow barked loudly. She either agreed with Mrs. Henry or just wanted a walk, I don't know.

Sighing, I thought to myself, *just another day in Westerly*!

"Wow, Katie," I said as Shadow and I walked over to see what was going on. "I never thought I'd see you helping Mrs. Henry with her chores!"

WB groaned. "I sure hate these messes you get me into," he groaned.

"Wow, WB," Katie replied. "I took your feet and

made them ride your skateboard. I never knew I had the talent to do that."

"Maybe I...I..."

"C'mon, you two, finish cleaning up the mess you made on my driveway," Mrs. Henry said. "Later you can curse each other," she continued.

Katie's face turned as red as the apple I ate for breakfast. "Aw, c'mon, Mrs. Henry," Katie said. "We didn't mean to make black marks on your driveway."

"I guess you both aren't in a hurry to go to the fireworks tonight," Mrs. Henry snickered. "You'll have your own fireworks right here, if you don't finish cleaning up those black marks before Greg gets home from work. Even Jules' God can't even save you!" she continued.

I shrugged my shoulders at Mrs. Henry's comment, now feeling a heavy weight on my shoulders. They felt as heavy as my book bag when my Math Teacher, Miss Scali gave us lots of homework.

"Sometime I...I..." Katie replied, ignoring the strange look I knew was on my face.

"Aw, c'mon, Katie," WB said. "Stop goofing and help me scrub."

You should've been there because me telling you the story isn't as great as seeing what we saw! The two of them, Katie and WB, were on their hands and knees! They were scrubbing black marks on the driveway! Marks which resembled balloon bike tires. Tire marks much like that of the bike laying in the Henry's front yard; Katie's purple bike.

Katie mumbled. I thought I heard her mention fireworks, but I'm not sure. It just sounded like it to me.

I grinned. "I'll catch you both later," I told my friends. "Please stay out of trouble. I'd hate for you to both miss the festival this year."

I thought I heard, "Humph!" from Katie, as Shadow and I walked away. I smiled to myself, knowing this time, it was meant for me. I smiled to myself, as we continued on our walk.

Yes, just another day in Westerly, Ohio!

I glanced at my watch. It was now 12:30pm. I couldn't believe my ears! I could still hear the blond mallard! There's actually a farm behind Katie's house!

Yep, we live on old farm land. We might live in the city, yet our area is rural.

There are a few old farmhouses on Moore. Moore is the road adjacent to our development. Rumor is the road was named after Junior Moore. Moore is the farmer that owns the blonde mallard duck. He also has chickens, a horse and even alpaca's! Did you know blond mallards are rare? I didn't until my brother Ed told me.

Mr. Moore sure put up a stink when they started building our development! He's nice to us kids, but he's always at council meetings. Yep, he complains whenever Fields Homes builds another home. He says they're taking the land from the animals. I agree, yet don't. I hate the fact that we humans are taking the land from the deer, but there wouldn't be a development named Deep Woods. And if there wasn't a Deep Woods, I wouldn't live in the sweet home I live in!

Our home has a huge backyard. We also have small hills on our property. The management of our development, Stern Management, calls this area, common area. They mow it, but we own and my parents pay taxes on it. I guess it works out. Ed doesn't have to mow that area. I know he's happy!

Hey, are you wondering where Ed is right now? I can see you nodding. He's at North Center Park. Ed, Jacob, and a few other guys, are playing baseball. I guess you can say Ed likes sports as much as I like reading. I heard he was pitching today. Ed has a closet full of sport cards and figures. Maybe that's another reason to come to our city, right? You can play ball or check-out Ed's collection. I heard his team is looking for a few good players.

Now, are you thinking Jules, you were talking about Blond mallards, how come you changed the subject and started talking about Ed? Hey don't be shy! I know I daydream and change the subject sometimes. Hey, give me a break! I'm 12 years old! But, hey I didn't fail! Ed reminds me of a blond mallard. A male mallard can be quiet, but they defend their territories. Mr. Moore's Blonde Mallard has waddled up to a neighbor's patio and squawked at his dog. Now, Ed, whom I described earlier, like the mallard, may be quiet at times. Yet, he can also be loud when he wants to be heard. When someone comes into our neighborhood trying to mess with any of his friends or family, Ed will stand up for us, and chase the intruder away. Yep, he likes to be the leader in most everything he does.

So, you thinking, "Here she goes again. She's not only daydreaming, but taking me into her daydream!"

It's alright if you're thinking this. Do you know what Ed's says if he thinks I'm going on and on? Yep, I'll tell you even if you don't want to know. *"Get to the point Jules. I don't have all day!"* So, if you think I'm doing just that, let me know. Do you think you could do that? Or you can just close the book and miss out on the big story, what happened in Westerly, Ohio.

"Please don't!" "My brother reminds me of a mallard and *"it's just another normal day in Westerly, Ohio!"*

The smoothing sound of the dryer could be heard from the laundry room. Friday was my day to wash clothes. I hated washing clothes. Especially Ed's clothes! And do you know why? I never know what I'd find in his pockets!

So, guess what I do? I don't check Ed's pockets anymore. Sure, once in a while the whites might turn pink. Or the whole load might have briars all over them. Hey, it's better than my hands having black glue all over it don't you think? Or smelling like one of Ed's old nasty socks. I'll tell you a secret if you promise not to tell Ed. Do you promise? Hey, you can at least say yes loud enough that I can hear you. Alright come over here close and for I can whisper it in your ear. "I just toss the ruined clothes in Ann's garbage." Hey, it saves me from my brother! So, do you have a better plan? If so, let me know alright?

"Woof! Woof'

Yep, Shadow was trying to get my attention. I stopped loading the washer to check on Shadow. She was looking out the window. Kneeling down on my knees next to her, I petted her smooth black head. I could now hear Mrs. Henry's voice and see something wasn't right on Rose Court.

Yep, again! It was Katie and WB. And I could see those grins. They rigged WB's skateboard to the back of Katie's bike and were riding past the Henry house.

Can you imagine the look on Mrs. Henry's face? Yep, you don't have to be a magician, and pop into my house! Again, remember that apple from this morning? I bet it wasn't as red as Mrs. Henry's face! And please recall I live across the street.

I just wish they'd stay out of trouble. Or just try to stay out of trouble for the rest of this weekend. Yep, I'd hate for my friends to miss the fun for a few minutes of dares. The Popcorn Festival is the last summer festival in our county. And in two weeks school would start and our summer vacation ended.

As I made my bed and straightened up my room, my thoughts lingered to North Center Park, my park. The park that not only housed the Popcorn Festival each year, but fun things all year long! I could close my eyes and vision the basketball hoops, tennis court; the hill Shadow and I love to run up-and-down. Did I tell you it's used for sledding in the winter months? Yes, just bring your sled. Close your eyes I bet you can imagine yourself sliding down a hill with that sled of yours. Can't you? How about dunking a basket or serving a tennis ball?

Yes, North Center Park is a fun place to hang out all year long. And if I haven't talked you into coming to visit yet, maybe I should tell you about the fishing pond. It's about 3 acres long. The city stocks it every year. And you don't need a fishing license to fish there either! There's a playground for younger children. The city even added a splash pad last year. It's open from the time school ends for the summer until we go back in the fall. The park has pavilion and grills. So, Moms and Dads, you can fish, walk, play sports and cook too, and it's all free! I guess if you aren't in your car now, I'd better get back to my story, right?

Hey, did you wonder where my parents are? Nope, I know you figured it out. You're right! They're at work. Yes, many of the parents in our neighborhood were either at work, or finishing their Friday running, to get ready for the festival. Not to talk for everyone, because only God can do that, and Jules Currier doesn't want His job! I have enough trouble doing my own, thank you! I, Jules Currier am excited to go to the festival tonight.

Yes I, like many folk in Westerly, Ohio, was having visions of carnival food in our heads. I bet your mouth is salivating! C'mon, who wouldn't salivate when thoughts of candy apples and fried cheese on a stick appeared in their head! Right! If not, how about frozen bananas, elephant ears, cabbage 'n noodles and don't forget Westerly popcorn? Come on fess up! You can't wait to come to Westerly, Ohio and join us, right? Hey, kids only get this stuff at carnivals, right? I doubt if there's a home in the whole world that has carnival food 24/ 7. If there was, I bet every kid in the world would want to live there. I would wouldn't you?

A few may, like me, have lingering thoughts of a game of chance. Or a pony ride. How about a ride on your favorite carnival ride? Mine is the Sizzler. What's yours?

Hey, did I tell you what our parents do while we are having fun at the festival? Get this, 'they just sit in the 'Adult tent!' I don't know why or what they do. I'll never hangout with them to find out either! I'd rather check-out the festival!

So, what do you think they do? Huh? I think they do boring stuff. They're old, so they don't know how to have fun. They probably talk about their day. A few may gossip about their kids. I know they miss all the stuff a festival has to give. Yep, they must miss the games, food, and good times.

Yes, WB and Katie do need to stay out of trouble. I'd hate to hear any kid had to miss out on the excitement.

Ann and I both had a date at the church tent. No, silly, not a real date. We promised Pastors Allen and Linch we'd help. I like hanging out with Ann, and she seems to like hanging with me. Helping Pastors Allen and Linch is an added bonus. I figure God's going to remember this, just in case we slip and do something wrong, though the Pastors have taught me God doesn't work like that.

You may not believe me but Ed promised to work a few hours too. I'm not sure which day. It'll just be sometime Saturday or Sunday. Yep, my brother might get into fixes, but he's a big believer in the 'Good Book," you know the bible. I think Ed might make a good preacher himself someday. Now he's just a kid. And I figure being a kid's a hard enough job. I just think my brother may be a future Pastor. Please don't tell him I said so. I don't think he's figuring to be one right now. Ed can talk himself out of a few situations. Yes, he will fess-up and take the consequences like all of us do. But he sure makes it hard on the adult to win in the situation!

Now, did you say, "Get to the point Jules? I don't have all day?" I know a few details in my story may seem boring at times, but don't close this book, and miss out on the entire story of what happens in Westerly, Ohio! I need to tell you a few details, or characters, plot, etc. I want to be writer or actor. Now back to my story...

"Fireworks..."

I again, for the hundredth t time today, rushed to the window.

Yep, it was Katie. Sure, I'm like the next kid; I do like seeing fireworks light the sky, but not being referred to so many times in one day! Yes, not comforting in the least!

The loveseat looked so inviting after my chores. I sat down. I opened my favorite book. Its title is, '*Brown*

Eyes.' It was written by Holly McCain. McCain has written two really funny books. Her books are written about her two pups, Shadow, Sadie and their friends. I know our pups, well mine and Ann's have the same names as Holly McCain's pups. She's my favorite author though and I've read a lot of books in my 12 years! Her work is not only amusing, but they remind me of Shadow and the things she does.

> '*Brown eyes stamped on our tomato plant.*
> *Brown eyes tore up my fancy pants.*
> *Brown eyes made Ma cuss and swear,*
> *she tore up her underwear.*
> *Brown eyes ...*

Chapter Three
Bad News for Katie

DING DONG!!...DING DONG!!

I guess I fell asleep. Yep, my doorbell was ringing. I rushed to answer it. I knew if I waited, Shadow would start barking. Now, don't say, "It's just a dog bark!" Shadow is a Labrador retriever mixed with a beagle. So, it's not just a bark. The sound is like "WOOF...H-O-W-L-!! WOOF...H-O-W-L!!" That pup maybe part Labrador retriever/beagle, but she's also part 'Woof Bell' too!

I opened the door. Looked up and blinked. *Huh?* I thought to myself. I mean, I thought I'd see Ann at the door. It was about 2:00pm and her class was probably over.

I blinked again. Hey, I didn't expect to see Mrs. Henry at the door! No, she still wore those work clothes. You know those shorts, baggy top and straw hat. I looked up at her face. Mrs. Henry was smiling. She didn't smile very much. I don't know why. Mrs. Henry has a beautiful smile. I bet my dentist would love her teeth! No, not weird love, but appreciate them. She'd even get a free bag of popcorn! My dentist gives children with good teeth in the months of July and August free tooth brush floss and a certificate for a free bag of popcorn from the Popcorn Factory. Yep, Mrs. Henry would get a free bag that's for sure! I, Jules Currier, well that's another story. Now back to Mrs. Henry.

"Can you tell me what time the fireworks start tonight, honey?" Mrs. Henry asked.

I gave Mrs. Henry a copy of our church bulletin. I knew this was the Henry's first year in Westerly. They moved here from a city in Chicago. Mrs. Henry works for our local vet office. She is an Animal Music Therapy Instructor. Yep, beside nice teeth, she's great with animals!

"Ostrander, Jeremy."

No, it's not a misprint. The phone was ringing. We have talking caller id. Mrs. Henry thanked me for the information and I ran to answer the phone. Are you still stuck on the talking caller id thing? Alright, I'll explain. The phone actually says who's calling, so we know whose calling before we answer it. The problem is, it repeats the name backwards. Ann's dads name is Jeremy Ostrander.

Ann gave me a brief description of what she did in woodturning class. She made her mom a sugar scoop.

Yep, I must explain the whole boring details. I promise I'll leave out some. Ann explained woodturning, because I didn't know what that was. Hey, do you? And you laughed at me! So, it's not turning a piece of wood around in your hands. How did I know! Ann, after giving me an Ann sigh, scared you just imagining it, right? I mean Ann enjoys woodworking, so I wasn't been a nice, laughing in her ear when she described the wood moving on a lathe, a machine holding the wood between two centers, which turns so the work can be shaped. I thought she said moving in a bath. You know bath instead of lathe, I guess she would've popped me right in my arm if she could reach me. This I know.

She told me she took a shower when she got home. I guess when you're woodturning, wood chips go everywhere. She found a few in her ears, hair and inside her shirt. We finished the conversation because of my laughter. Ann is really serious when it comes to woodworking. I guess my last joke about wood chips wasn't funny to her. So, let's see what you think, alright?

First, imagine, you're a great magician. Now, instead of producing a coin from your ear, you pull a nice chunk of wood. The applause from the crowd fills the auditorium. The crowd loves you! You're booked for the rest of the year or until your parents make you clean your ears out, and then your career ends. You're sent to an ear specialist. I know! I know!

"Get to the point Jules? I don't have all day?"

"Hey Jules..."

I glanced out the window. There was Katie and

WB smiling up at me. Behind them I caught a glimpse of a few other kids, even Ann. Ann must have forgiven me for laughing about her woodworking class. What do you think? I don't hear you! Katie had the skateboard and WB Katie's bike. Katie attempted a kick flip. She almost fell flat on her face. A person kicks the board with the ball of the foot. After the board spins and flips at least once the skateboarder tries to land on it. Yep, Katie missed.

"What's up?" I yelled back. I wanted to read my book or maybe watch television. I had the remote in one hand and book in the other. I didn't have a hand to wave at the gang.

"We're heading to our hill; do you want to come with us?" WB asked.

I smirked. "I'll be out in one minute." I opened the garage door jumping on my bike. I took off before my garage door fully shut.

We were on the way to the hill.

Chapter Four
Our Hill

The Hill located a street from my house was our spot. I guess someday that hill will be a house, but for now it's our hangout. We ducked around the corner looking behind us to make sure nobody saw us going to our meeting place. I don't know why we do it, but we do it every time we meet. We can meet seven times a day! It's not like our parents don't know about "The Hill." We always let them know where we are. It's just the thrill of doing kid stuff. I know you've done something like this, right? Now don't lie and say you haven't. I know everyone lies a time or two. I guess God knows we are kids and part of being kids is telling a little fib once-in-awhile. But we're all kids' right; and we kids stick together, right? So, how about telling me you pretend too, right?

THUD! THUD! I could hear something, or someone coming up our hill. I closed my eyes. I felt something on my trembling foot. Ann's butt was on it! I could feel wetness on my face. *Come on body, calm down! We need to save our hill.* My body didn't seem to hear my thoughts, yes, sweat poured down my favorite purple shirt.

The steps drew closer. Ed always tells me to stand up to fears, but could I? Eyes damp, from fear, and closed tight as a clam shell, my trembling hands reached for a rock, which conveniently lay beside me. I tried to stand up. Sure, maybe I could if Ann would move her butt! Talking about foot, my damped eyes, now partially open, saw a huge pair right beside me. *Jules don't fear. God your Father is always there,* I thought to myself. Instead of running, I smiled. I learned smiling and laughing can sometimes help me through tense situations.

I glanced up into the hazel eyes of our monster. He

34

stood at least 6"7; he wore dirty blue jeans, a plaid shirt.

So this is what it feels like in your last moments? I thought to myself. *Bad! Of course it would be better if Ann would get her butt off my right foot! I must be brave. Still, on the pain scale of 1 to 10 my foot now was a 10.*

I guess it is time to pray. Did you ever notice most people pray when you're in trouble?

"What do you want?"

I first thought, *Wow God, you came fast! After all, I just asked him for help didn't I? But it was WB's voice. Still, I wasn't complaining.*

I glanced towards WB. He was glaring at the man like "I'm the man!"

Unfortunately, the man didn't budge. He didn't smile. He didn't talk. I held back one of my smiles. Now, I've got to admit, I was a little frightened. Now, just a little.

Finally, WB picked up a rock. The rock in my clenched hand was now wet. Our brave friends' rock landed at least 2 feet away. I assume it fell into a field. *Great, what should we do? God,* I prayed to myself, *you do remember seeing me in church last Sunday, right? I'm going in a few days. I promise.*

"Psst... Jules," Katie whispered. "I haven't prayed in a long time. I know you do. Can you help me pray?"

I whispered back, "Sure, Katie."

"I-I-I am afraid," Katie whispered. "I wish I was my favorite animal, a skunk. I wouldn't be so afraid."

I whispered back, "I love deer. I wouldn't want to be one, but I understand."

I whispered a short prayer. God doesn't care if a prayer is short or long. He loves us.

WB took now soaked rock from my hand. Then he shouted. "What do you want?" he repeated.

All was silent. Well, all but the loud rocking beat of my heart. The monster reached over and took the rock from WB's hand. My body shook as a **THUNDER** of laughter filled my ears. There's only one way to describe this...it wasn't a small laugh, but a roar!

CRUNCH! RUMBLE! ROAR! Another sound approached.

"Hey kids, you need a new place to hang-out." Mr. Appletree said. "The bulldozers are approaching. We're going to build a house here. And what did you think I was, a monster or something?" he continued laughing. "And Waterbury, I'd watch threatening people with rocks," he continued.

We laughed. A monster! Sure, he might have monsters for kids, but what did he think we were, two years old? Monster, yeah right!

Now, are you still laughing at WB's name? Hey, kids don't have a choice what their name's going to be. WB, named after his Great-grandfather, has stood up to much teasing.

Firmly, yet still a little unsteady (from Ann's butt which was now off my foot), I stood up. Shaking the cramp from my foot, I turned to the others. "I need to get home. The bathroom is mine. I'd like to keep it mine before Ed claims it!"

It was always a joke that I was a little bit too neat. Everyone thought Ed's way of doing things was right and I was 'much too clean'.

We said goodbye all glancing back at the hill. Bulldozers now covered the space we left. I knew the workers were only doing their job, but it still hurt. In what seemed like autopilot, I rode home, or my bike took me towards home. I unconsciously wiped a tear from my eye. I felt sad. We lost something important. Sure, we'd find a new spot. But change can be hard. I could see Mrs. Henry, who was now watering her bushes, flowers and trees when I rode past her house. I waved my hand, not caring if Katie got mad seeing my friendly gesture.

Unconsciously, I put my bike into the garage, and opened the door. Shadow welcomed me at the door, so did the blinking of the answering machine. I petted Shadow and touched the button on the answering machine that read, 'Play."

Ann's voice came on. "I'm wearing my favorite capris and that bright pink shirt Pastor Allen gave us. What you wearing?"

I, myself, was wearing my favorite black shorts and the forbidding pink shirt. I didn't know what the rest of the kids were wearing. We'd soon find out when we met later at the gazebo.

Cleaning up, my mind wandered to last year's festival. Everyone, surely, enjoyed themselves. I know I did! I tugged on my shorts and adjusted my pink shirt.

*I will **NOT** think of our hill tonight.* I promised myself. *I will have an awesome time!*

Chapter Five
The Popcorn Festival

The familiar smells and sites of a festival awakened my senses, that August day. I could smell popcorn mixed with smells of hotdogs and cotton candy. Festival workers were setting up their booths. A distance away, I saw the Graviton whiz through the air. The

Graviton is a rite of passage ride. What I mean is you stop riding The Ferris Wheel, a Mom and Dad ride, to defy gravity.

Yellow tape with the word "**CAUTION**" showed drivers Northridge, or the part where the festival was being held, closed to traffic. So, if you want to go to Westerly Library, you must park in the festival parking lot and walk to library. I know the Appletree's, wouldn't be real happy about the closed road or the festival either. Brenda Appletree, whom reminds me of old sour milk, you know, after it's sat in the fridge too long, didn't like to walk. Yeah, when the Appletrees' weren't happy, Mayor McClaren wasn't happy. And the Appletrees' live in our development.

Brenda likes to go to the library. She knows Justin Baker uses the computers there. Yeah, Brenda likes Justin Baker. I'm not really sure Justin likes her, but he gets to ride her Dad's bulldozer, so he'll even like Brenda.

No, I'm not going off in my 'Jules daydreaming'! Well, maybe I'm going on about Brenda Appletree, a bit too much, but what am I supposed to do, she just walked by sticking her tongue out at me. I heard her whisper under her breath, "Your precious hill is gone!"

I tried to not stick my tongue out. I've learned in my 12 years, it's best to ignore people. I smiled to myself. Smiling seems to help me when times are tough and you know this time was **VERY** tough! And also, it makes Brenda so mad when I smile, so that makes it even better, right?

"I expect you both to meet me here after the fireworks," Mom's words made my thought snap away from Brenda Appleseed.

"Ok, Mom."

"Jules..."

"And don't forget to eat."

"Ok, Mom." I said stumbling to keep up with Ann 'long-legs.'

I smiled. I knew if I didn't run a little faster, Mom would give me her long lectures on 'having a good, healthy meal.' And Ann would beat me to the church tent. Bright pink shirts, identical to mine and Ann's, could be seen a few yards away.

Pastor Allen and Linch must be putting up the tent, I thought to myself. *It's nice to see Pastors, Mayors, etc. are human, do live life outside their job.* They go to movies, stores, and festivals. I forget they're human sometimes. Do you? Let's face it, there are certain things **ALL** of us do:

- We eat.
- We drink.
- We sleep.
- We brush our teeth.
- We yawn.
- We fart (yes, even Pastors!)
- We use the bathroom (yes, even Teachers!).

This is reality. But I guess, we sometimes forget and think to put these people on pedestals. But there's one thing to think the next time Miss Scali or Miss or Mr., whoever your teacher is looks at you like, you're from another planet:

She or he is human. They eat, drink, sleep, brush their teeth, yawn, fart and use the bathroom, just like you and me.

Of course, I don't want you getting in trouble laughing at this as you read this book, but I just thought I'd tell you the truth. And I did.

C-RASH!!

I staggered trying to see why there were fireworks in my world, when it wasn't even 9:00pm yet!

"Hey," Brenda Appletree shouted; "Watch where you're going!"

The big jerk, well she stands 6"1' to my 4"10' body, stood above my star glazed head. I guess I won't lie by saying I was happy at the moment and didn't have some choice cuss words in my throbbing head at the moment, so I won't.

Fortunately, after recalling a few bars of soap, I kept those words to myself. It was really hard. Part of me wanted to tell the jerk, what I thought. I tell you, God knew what I was thinking, and knew how really tough it was for me not to say them. Fortunately, I bit my tongue.

I wasn't sure what Brenda Appletree said next, Ann grabbed my arms and helped me up on my feet. "Come on!" she whispered. "Even your God can't save you right now Jules!" I felt heaviness on my body. My body felt like I fell off my bike, but worse. Also, wasn't this the second time today someone used God and I in the same sentence? Didn't Mrs. Henry say something similar? I shrugged my shoulders and painfully continued walking to serve.

The walk seemed to take forever! My body felt sore all over. *What's wrong with me?* I thought to myself. The rest of our walk went without any more problems, or was there? The two of us finally made it to the church tent. But I felt like something really strange was going on. Well, first my pink tee shirt is now torn. It seems that when I fell, the friction from both the movement and ground tore my shirt. You don't need to be a rocket scientist to imagine the dilemma I was in! But there was something more! I shrugged and followed Ann into the church tent.

Pastor Linch glanced at my shirt and at my face. "I'm not going to ask." she whispered. "There's another one your size in tub in the back of tent. Just go to the bathroom and change.' Without a word, I walked to the back of the tent and picked out another shirt. I looked over my shoulder and noticed Ann whispering to Pastor Linch. I knew she was telling her what happened. I'm sure she told her the whole story. She just didn't add one thing, my head was aching and I didn't want to see that big lug Brenda Appletree anymore that night. I knew deep in my heart I wouldn't and couldn't keep those cuss words in me much longer. I'm sure there'd be a nice bar of soap waiting for me at home if I did say them out loud.

In a matter of seconds, I changed tee shirts, dropping

the torn one into the trash can, with more strength then I should've. I knew if I just put the shirt into the trash, I'd walk away with all the anger and frustration still in me. If I dropped it in the trash, I'd be letting out some of the stuff built up in me, and I'd return to the tent, ready to start the evening over. So, I had chosen the latter. Now I was ready to go back to the tent and do my job.

I wonder what Jesus would do in my circumstance, I thought to myself. *He'd smile to himself and go back to serving others.* I flashed myself and whoever could see me a grin, and walked back towards the church tent. It was only a few dozen of yards from where the festival latrine or bathroom was. I figured that I'd look at a few stands on the way back. I knew this little bit of time would be just the thing to make me forget about her. You know, what's her name?

There were stands with food, like elephant ears, and taco salad. There were crafts, like jewelry and clothing. Again, there were more stands of food, yeah, Sloppy Joes, deep fried onions and corn on the cob. Great! I didn't look at the food to make me hungry, I did it to forget. I'd just get something later.

At last, I reached the church tent. I pulled a stick of gum out of my front shorts pocket. Unwrapping, my sweet treat, I put it in my mouth longingly. (*I just pray my stomach stops growling. I will get something to eat later.*)

"She's here!" Ann cried

I glanced towards my best friend and smirked. "What's up?" I asked. She smirked back. "We're doing the children's games this year!" she said.

She walked towards the "fishing game," leaving me to follow. I smiled and followed my best friend to the game. There was a small swimming pool filled with water. There were plastic fish of different colors floating amongst each other. I knew each fish had a different number on it. Every number would win a child a prize, but one fish would have a number on it that would win a lucky child a bigger prize!

"Hi there," I said, walking up to each family that approached our tent. "Would your child like to try…?"

It was a long, but fun evening for me. Ann and I not only gave away a lot of stuff, we also helped the church get new visitors. So, Ann and I, or rather I, since I can't speak for Ann, was happy. Don't get me wrong, Ann seemed to be having as much fun as I was, but I learned in the last 12 years you don't speak for someone else. They have their own thoughts and feelings.

8:00 P.M. Rides. Or, should we get food or play games? I'm telling you, being a kid is tough! You know how it is, because you're one too! It's like you wish someone could tell you what to do, but you'd rather make some decisions yourself. I wish God put a gadget on us that we could press and it would make the decision. My parents would tell me God puts it in our heart. I wish God puts it in my heart soon, because Jules is having a hard time deciding.

I noticed a crowd beginning to form around a table. "I wonder what's going on." I asked.

"I don't know." Ann mumbled.

I glanced over to where the crowd was gathered. For a second, I thought of just turning the other way and going to find food, but for some reason... I felt magnetized to the table.

"I need to eat something, soon," Ann called behind me.

"Come on Ann, can't you keep up?"

"I thought short people walked slower!" "Slow down Jules!" Ann continued.

I figured that Ann had two choices…either follow me to the table or turn around and go get something to eat. It was her choice, I didn't care right then. I just needed to get to that table! I don't know…sometimes you just have to go with your gut feeling and do something even if your friends or family try to get in the way. And this was just one of those times!

I suppose when you read this it's like your saying, *Hey Jules just get to the point. What's at that table?* But heck, I'm writing this right? So, you can either read it or go get something to eat, right?

With a deep breath I pushed myself through the crowd, using my 4'10" body to go under a few arms.

For a moment I thought I was dreaming! I know the expression of shock registered on my face. I know I needed to yell to the whole the world the great news, but like I said, I was just standing in stupidity.

Ann caught up with me. And then, before I knew it, I was standing face to face with my favorite author, Holly McCain. She was signing her latest book, "Puppy Love," and her first book, "Brown Eyes."

McCain's work is not only clever, but awesome! Hey, the lady takes poetry to a whole new level! It's not only easy and fun to read, she captures the attention of us kids, an impressive task I'd say!

"Please, God," I prayed quietly, "don't let me fart or Ann belch." (Ann has a history of burping anytime and anywhere.)

I don't know whether it was my gasp or because she happened to look up at the time, but Holly McCain was looking me right straight into my face!

She put her hand out to me, "Hi, I'm Holly McCain, author of the Puppy Poetry books, "Brown Eyes" and "Puppy Love."

My shaking knees moved like the dryer this morning. And my hands were as wet as the clothing I took out of the washing machine. And my favorite author, the famous Holly McCain, wanted to shake my hand!

I put my right hand out towards hers. Unfortunately, it was still dripping with sweat. Ms. McCain didn't seem to notice or let on like some kid just got sweat all over her writing hand.

Finally, it registered. I just shook hands with Holly McCain! My mouth felt like the black glue from Ed's pants pockets was in my mouth. *Please lips don't let me down,* I thought to myself! Trying real hard to make my lips move, I managed to say "H-hello." I guess the next few words are what Ann told me, because I don't remember. I was out cold. She told me that I had dropped to the ground like when Brenda Appletree knocked me over. How embarrassing!

Ann told me that Ms. McCain asked her other fans to please step back and she literally carried me to the back of her tent. Ann, a science fiction fan, is now a fan of Holly McCain too! She usually doesn't read poetry books, "We have to read enough of that in school!" she complained. "But I was just wondering. When you're done with her books, could I read them?" Ann asked.

"Sure," I answered. I could still feel my flushed face. *I know my face looked like the apple I had for breakfast.*

A half hour later and after Ms. McCain thought I was alright, Ann and I were on our way to get something to eat. We only had around 30 minutes before we'd be meeting the rest of our friends at the gazebo.

"Come on, Jules," Ann said, grinning, "Before you get yourself into another fix. I'm starving!"

Maybe it was from fainting or getting knocked over

by the Big Lug, Brenda Appletree, or because I was real hungry! I looked over at Ann. Ann looked at me. "FOOD!" we both shouted in unison!

The air was filled with the smell of deep-fried fat from the many booths at the festival. Funnel cakes… French fries…Grilled sausage with peppers and on-ions…Cotton Candy…Popcorn. Yes, Popcorn! And you may find buttery corn on the cob. Or even cabbage and noodles cooked in lots of butter. Yes, cabbage and noodles, I found what I was having. Ann got in line at the grilled chicken booth. We'd both get ears of corn and nice large lemonade before meeting the gang.

"BELCH! BELCH!"

"You're gross," I groaned, after Ann did her after meal burps. She explained, when we first met, that it is a family habit. If the meal was good, it was a com-pliment to the chef. I shook my head, looking around to see if anyone heard my friend…

"Hey, aren't you even going to excuse yourself?"

We spun around at the same time, almost knocking each other over. It was Dennis "The Whacko" Apple-tree. Yes, all 6' 200lbs of him! Both Dennis and Ann looked like they wanted to smash each other's face into the ground whenever they see each other.

"I said, aren't you going to excuse yourself, belch face?"

Everyone in the festival seemed to be looking. It felt like every pair of eyes was on us.

Ann's face was as red as the sign on the Zipper, the ride right across from us. If you never been on the Zipper, you've missed out! The Zipper rotates like the Ferris wheel, but so different! The Zipper has 12 passenger cages, which fit two adult sized people. Riders are seated in odd shaped capsules. The capsules are evenly apart like the rows of the zipper on your coat. You ride in circles so fast, the capsules can rotate clock wise and counter-clockwise! Ann can't handle the Zipper. She can't handle any ride! She says if she wanted to get dizzy and puke her guts out, she'd find better ways, thank you!

I'm getting away from my subject again, "The Whacko." He goes to the local psycho place, Knickerbockers Center. He has what society calls, "Anger Management Problems." His anger doesn't seem to be managed whenever he sees Ann! Yes, my friends, whenever he sees her, he wants to imprint her head into the pavement. I could feel my heart up in my throat. I feared for Ann. I didn't want my best friend to be part of the Senior Center parking lot forever! I bet you my friends feel the same way, right?

"THEY'RE OVER HERE!" Austin yelled.

I was about to drag my dear, friend away from the situation myself, but Austin, Ed, Jacob and the gang were heading our way. In his true bully ways, Whacko threw Ann a look that packed harder than any old punch! Ann threw him a goodbye, "BELCH!"

Fortunately for me, the gang arrived and my mouth dropped back in place.

"Hey, are you two having any problems?" Ed yelled from his spot under the gazebo.

"I don't think so, just, a few words with W-H-A-C-K-O!" Ann replied.

"Shut up!" I gasped.

"You shut up!"

"Will you two both just come on?" Katie growled. "You've already made us wait for 20 minutes. Let's get to our spot."

"Sorry everyone," I mumbled. "It's been a L-O-N-G day!"

"Maybe you can tell us later." Katie growled.

I was irritated. Not only was my best friend a pig, but also the look Katie had just given me, was like it was I, Jules Currier, who held up things. And of course, if you asked dear, Ann, she would probably say the same thing. And little did we ALL know; life would be changing for ALL of us! Yes, VERY, VERY soon!

Once we all got together, Katie, WB, Jacob, Austin, Ed, Ann and I, all the stress seemed to disappear. We started laughing and nudging each other.

As the time got closer to 'Fireworks Time,' more people filled North Center Park. I saw many familiar faces. Pastors Linch and Allen could be seen in their spot under the gazebo. Mr. and Mrs. Kordic were under their favorite tree on the hill. Shadow (Mom must of went home & got her), were near the Kordic's. Mr. McClaren was close by. Yep, there were parents, a few classmates, and Brenda and Dennis Appletree. Oh No! A few feet away stood the Henry's and their cat, Francois.

I nudged Ann with my arm.

"No way!" she whispered.

The rest of the gang heard her whisper. Ann's whispers are more like talking.

Perfect. The Appletree's and the Henry's were standing together. All our enemies were gathered together! The thought made my body hurt.

Brenda Appletree whispered something to Wacko. He smirked and looked at Ann.

Shadow whined to get to me. Mrs. Kordic smiled and brought her over.

And, of course, that made me feel a lot better! Shadow always makes me feel safe and content!

I petted her head, until she gave my hand a lick. Everything would be alright, or would it?

Mayor McClaren announced that the fireworks would begin in 10 minutes.

K-BOOM! POP! K-BOOM!

Shadow hid between my legs. Poor girl! I wondered why Mom brought her here and where my Mom was!

Did you know that fireworks are fired around 800 feet into the sky? Ann told me this. The fire department, or whoever is doing the display, can't set off fireworks if there is any wind, which there wasn't. The people, who set off the fireworks, wear fluorescent jackets to so the crowd can see them a distance away. The jackets are needed for the viewers (us), can identify them, for safety reasons. Yes, another bit of knowledge from Ann.

K-BOOM! POP! K-BOOM!

Poor Shadow trembled. I'd have to talk to my Mom about bringing her to this. She knows how she gets frightened by sounds. Can you smell the smoke?

Suddenly, the sky lit up with light. Please close your eyes real tight. Can you imagine the sky lit up by the awesome lights? Can you? Please yell YES!

W-HIZ!

CRACK!

SNAP!

K-BOOM!

"A-H-H-H-H-H..."

"O-O-H..."

"W-h-o-o-s-h!" I felt the friction of someone or something glazing over my painful shoulder. Looking around I could see Katie walking towards Mrs. Henry.

Oh, no, I thought to myself, rubbing my shoulder. *What is Katie up to?*

W-W-IZ!

Next, the worst explosion of my life! And re-member, I'm 12 years old! I first thought it was my own heart just leaping out of my chest from the loud sounds. I guess it's never too young for a heart attack.

Next, what happened will change Westerly forever in my eyes! And in the eyes of my gang, neighbors, and maybe even you!

Blackness filled the sky, yes tar-black as dark as the glue in Ed's pockets. Do you remember I told you about it when I was washing clothes this morning? Please yell **YES**! Please close your eyes real tight. Do you see darkness? Please say **YES**!

"I am the light of the world. Whoever follows me will never walk in darkness, but will have the light of life." I know things are looking tuff and I'm remembering a verse from John 8:12 in my Bible. Could you pray for me, my dear friends? I'm just afraid, and need you. I wonder if prayers would help now. *Why is it getting darker?* I thought to myself. *And why am I in so much pain?*

'**Y-O-O-O**!' A cry filled the air. The hair on my head and arms were sticking up.

"OUCH!" I yelled. It felt like pieces of firecracker was pounding my skin! My skin burnt from what I now knew was hail.

Next I could hear a loud **H-U-M**; much like the sound of bees could be heard. "**B-O-O-M,**" no, my friends, it wasn't fireworks! The sounds of wind and rain chocked my 12 year old body. And rain harder than any bathtub shower could ever make!

Now, the way I figured it, I could either run, which most people were doing. Or I could close my eyes and find out this was all a dream.

"LOVE YOUR NEIGHBOR AS YOURSELF," a voice roared from the skies, much like a loud crash of

thunder, God's word from the book of Matthew 22:39 (NIV) Bible could be heard. *"HOWEVER, IF YOU DO NOT OBEY THE LORD YOUR GOD AND DO NOT CAREFULLY FOLLOW ALL HIS COMMANDS AND DECREES I AM GIVING YOU TODAY..."* the loud voice continued, now from Deuteronomy 28:15 (NIV) Bible.

Chapter Six
Deer Me

"No, *no*, *no!*" I screamed as I woke that Saturday morning.

I not only had the strangest feeling. I've always had a good sense of smell, but, it's crazy, because it seemed so much better than usual! I could smell something else. I smelled...

"What are you yelling about?" asked Ann.

I opened my eyes, shut them, and then reopened them. My best friend was flying around the room. Yes, I repeat, **FLYING** around the room! She had wings! My best friend was not human. She was an Eagle!

"I'm hungry, you don't happen to have any fish in your fridge do you?" Ann asked.

I also had a craving for grass. Yes, the grass that Ed mowed each week! Boy, I must just be dreaming because I also feel like my ears are much too big for my face! And my tail was down. Tail, what am I saying? People don't have tails, but I have a tail! I have a deer tail! And my best friend doesn't become an Eagle over-night!

I looked down at my own body. I rubbed my eyes and let out the biggest, "NO," ever!

"She awoke." Ed's voice could be heard in the hall outside my room. "I'm surprised I didn't wake her at 4:00am."

Oh my…..! My brother is a blond mallard! You know the kind that quacks and struts around the pond!

"Has she seen Shadow yet?" Ed the blond mallard asked Ann the eagle.

I stood up, or tried to stand up. It's a little bit tough. You don't always turn into a real live deer, or fawn over night!

Ann and Ed were laughing. I bet you are laughing too, right?

"This is NOT funny," I said. "And I'm NOT dreaming either." "I am a fawn. Ann is an eagle. Ed is a blond mallard. And Shadow is the Mayor of Westerly!"

Yes, Shadow or her new form stood in my doorway. My pal was now the Mayor of Westerly! She was a he! But even bigger, the **PUP** was a **HUMAN**! And not only a **HUMAN**, but a **MAYOR**!

"This is **IMPOSSIBLE**!" I moaned out loud.

"You're right, Jules...it is impossible." Ann remarked as I rubbed my eyes again. "So, let's just enjoy this dream while we are in it, ok? I'm hungry. Hey, Shadow, is there any fish downstairs in that kitchen? I don't want to have to eat blond mallard for breakfast!"

"You think you have a chance? Obviously too much

blood has rushed into that Eagle brain of yours!" shrieked Ed.

"STOP!" I yelled.

"AHHHHHHHhhhhhh…"

We all ran, or tried to run, fly or whatever to my bedroom window. What we saw more than a dream, it was a cartoon! There was a cat chasing a skunk across the street at the Henry's house in the hail, rain and lightning. Yes, it was hail as large as golf balls. And not only some skunk chasing the cat, but the skunk had Mrs. Henry's voice!

"Hey move over and let me see." Shadow said in a bark like voice.

I stared at my pal. Yes, this dream was going to be kind of fun. My pal could talk. I could find out different things about her. We could communicate in our own way. But now, we actually could talk to each other!

"NO! Don't you try to kiss me, you CAT!" Mrs. Henry screamed.

First things first, though. We had to help bring

peace to the Henry's. But…I needed to take some gentle steps. I couldn't just leap out the window, now could I? And remember, Jules Currier is afraid of storms.

"NO! NO! NO!" Mrs. Henry screamed. "This is NOT real! I'm not a skunk! You're not a cat! Francois is NOT a human! No, no, NO!"

"*Oh, my goodness!*" whispered Ann. "What are we going to do?"

"Have fun in our God appointed bodies!" Ed replied.

I stared from the blond mallard to the eagle to the human. I reached over and hugged Shadow, or the Mayor. "We'll talk later." I whispered for only her or he could hear.

Shadow didn't say a word, just hugged me back.

"Hey, let's just see what we can do for the Henry's." I laughed. I trust I won't get hurt by the lightening.

"Greg!" snapped Mrs. Henry. You are NOT a CAT! I'm NOT a SKUNK! This is a DREAM! Leave me alone!"

"That's no way to talk to your husband, Skunk or no skunk." Mr. Henry laughed.

Not wanting to listen to him or live in this 'dream,' the skunk lifted her tail and blasted her foul mist. The cat, prepared for the attack, pounced out of the way.

"Shhh!" hushed the cat with paw over the skunk's mouth. "Let's go inside away from the hail, rain and lightning, before we have all the neighbors outside our house!"

"I don't care about the neighbors nor or the weather!" the skunk shouted or tried to shout. The cat gently, but urgently, guided the skunk towards the front door. We tried to keep ourselves away from the skunk's tail. Yep, her foul smell still lingering in the air.

"Good idea, Greg," Shadow said, as the Mayor, whom now stood with the front door open.

"No!" Mr. Henry shouted. "The dog's a person!"

The cat gently guided the skunk past the person and into the house. "Won't you all follow us in?" Mr. Henry asked. "Oh, watch your step though. There are broken glasses and dishes all over the kitchen!" he added.

You could tell the skunk was breathing hard. I guess it was easy. I could hear the breaths. I looked over at Ann and smiled. Her eyes were fixed on the skunk's tail. All our eyes were focused on that tail. The cat seemed to notice it too.

"Now, Lorraine, we're in the house. I like you to express your opinion, but your opinion may take months, maybe years to get out of our house." he said soberly.

All our attention was still drawn to the skunk, or to her tail.

I swallowed hard. My gentle mouth resumed its chewing motion. The skunk noticed this.

"Do you have to keep chewing?" she shouted.

"I can't help it!" I stated. "I'm a fawn, and this is what fawn's do."

"Jules Currier?" gasped Mrs. Henry. "You're a deer!"

"I'm actually a fawn. A young deer and my brother's a blond mallard. My pal's a Mayor. And my best friend's an eagle. My neighbors are a skunk and cat.

Their cat is a human! We are all living the same night-mare. What -"

"NO! NO! NO!"

Our conversation was interrupted by the sound of the loudest shout. We all ran, flew, crawled, whatever, to the Henry's window. Outside the Almost home on Willow Tree Court, where Katie Almost lives, stood Mrs. Henry, or Mrs. Henry's body. Well, Mrs. Henry with Katie Almost's voice that is!

"I don't believe it…" the skunk shrugged. "I'm a skunk, and that kid has my body!"

A voice interrupted her thoughts. "Shouldn't we go help her?" the cat asked. "And remember, dear," he said to the skunk. "She has your body and ALL the pains that go with it!" he continued.

"Hey, you're right!" the skunk said in what seemed like triumph. "Hey, Old lady, shouldn't you get some clothes on more your age? And ones that fit!"

A butterfly landed on Mrs. Henry's shoulder. The skunk tried to brush the butterfly off, but it wouldn't leave. The butterfly whispered something in her ear.

The expression on Mrs. Henry's face showed surprise, or what would look like surprise on a skunks face. I looked at the butterfly. It was a beautiful monarch.

By now, you and I both know this butterfly was Pastor Linch.

"We don't have time for teasing, dear. Why don't you go into the house and watch this from the window?"

"And miss all the fun?" the skunk replied, trying to again make the butterfly go away.

The cat gently, but firmly, guided the skunk back across the street. We turned back towards the Almost home. Katie, or Katie in Lorraine Henry's body, was still wearing the outfit she wore the night before. Please don't laugh too loud readers; I know this is rather funny; I'm trying not to laugh myself. But, here's a 60 some year old lady wearing a 10 year olds clothing! And they not only don't fit, but look ridiculous on her! And she was soaked!

"NO! NO! NO!" the angry and confused Katie yelled.

Ann tried to rub her chin, or where her chin used to

be, with her wing. She almost fell in flight. "Hmmm, I guess it will take a little while to get use to everything!'

"I need answers!" Katie demanded. "Why am I that old lady? Why is she a skunk? Why is her husband a cat? The cat's her husband, right? And is that you, Jules? You're a deer! And is your brother a blond mallard? Hey, Ann, did you know you're an eagle? And Mayor McClaren, you'd better fix this before my parents get home. My dad's a cop and he's gonna be real mad when he gets home. He might even hurt me before he even figures out who I am!"

"Actually, I'm a fawn and this is..." I replied.

Shadow broke into a huge grin before I could finish what I was going to say. "Ha! And you want me to do what?"

"What?" said Katie with arms held high. "Who are you?"

"I'm Shadow!" Shadow laughed. "I believe this is going to be so much fun!" she or he said.

"You're not funny!" the angry woman shouted.

Shadow was still laughing. Her laughter seemed to

help release all the tension in all of us. The air was filled by people, eagle, butterfly, blond mallard and fawn laughter. Yep, even Katie's laughter echoed from the house in Deep woods Development in Latrain County.

Ann flew down and mischievously said, "So, Katie, how does it feel to be the oldest not the youngest amongst us?"

'Eat a dead carcass, Eagle!" Katie teased. It was funny just hearing this come from the body of Lorraine Henry, or a body I thought was hers.

"Whose, yours skunk?" Ann teased back.

Great anxiety, fear, and confusion seemed to be released from all. I took a deep breath. These were my friends. They might not look like my friends, brother, pup; but they were. And I don't know what was happening, but we would figure it out. Yeah, it was just fun and quite comical to be together as we were: Human, Blond mallard, Eagle, and Deer.

"Ed, was I dreaming, or were you or another blond mallard splashing in the pond behind my bedroom window 4:00 a.m. this morning?" Katie asked.

"Hey, it's not every day that a boy wakes up a blond mallard! I had to let everyone know! Plus, ducks don't care about rain, hail or lightning." Ed exclaimed.

Shocked, but not really shocked, I looked at my brother the blond mallard. "You didn't?" I asked.

"I don't have time for lectures, dear sister." the blond mallard replied. 'I have to meet my new friends, Jordan and Franklin. They're domestic or normal mallard ducks." And my brother took off towards the Almost's back yard.

Ann sighed. "You think he'll be alright, or should I go look for my next meal in the Almost's yard?"

"My brother's tough!" I laughed. "He'll teach those mallards and geese a thing or two!"

Everyone started laughing.

My hunger for grass got to me. I started eating a few buds off the Almost's apple tree.

"NO!" shrieked Katie. "I believe I have enough to worry about. My Dad might mace me before he knows I'm not Mrs. Henry. I don't need the additional problem of you eating Mom's apple tree."

"You're probably right." I said turning towards the back of the Almost's property. "There's some nice hay and maybe some corn near Ed's pond. See you all later." My attention was now drawn to finding something to eat. The morning sun was heating my back, and I knew I had a few 'fawn' body things to do too.

Fawns or deer can adapt to almost all habitat, so I quickly, but quietly slipped into the farm yard. I could hear the commotion in the duck pond. A lone horse shared hay with me. The horse, Pastor Allen and I filled our guts with fresh hay. We both knew and believed God was watching over us, and we would be all alright in our own skin, hair, and feathers. I trusted God. I would be safe. My body seemed to feel a little different with this thought. I'm not sure what was happening, but I felt something inside change.

After a little chat and filling my paunch or gut with hay, I left the horse, Pastor Allen. I spent the next few hours in the field, doing what deer do, chewing my cud, or the apple buds, hay, oak, acorns and all I had collected. **PLEASE**, I will not explain how I had re-swallowed everything I ate. You the reader can just say, **YUCK**, and get it over with. God didn't give deer the same digestive system as a human. Humans have gallbladders to help their food digest. A few like the deer don't have gallbladders. So, the food goes through four chambers in the body. Another problem, a deer needs to pee around thirteen times a day, so...

Later, back at my home, the Currier home, I wandered into the garage. I'd left the garage door open earlier, or I believe I did. So, I slipped into the garage, closing the door with my hoof. Shadow must have heard me coming in because her, or her in her Mayor's body, opened the door for me.

I stood a moment, not believing, twenty-four hours ago, I was Jules Currier, a human. Yes, twenty-four hours ago, one day ago, I was getting ready for the Popcorn Festival. And you wonder what can happen in a day!

"He turned their rain into hail, with lightning throughout their land." Psalms 105-32 filled my heart.

"Uh, Jules, you need to see this!" Ann called from the living room.

"We have breaking news from Westerly. Reports of a dog playing golf with hail shaped golf balls. And a skunk was seen driving a van, with a cat steering, have filled our telephone lines, emails, and text messages. Just in, a horse with

a butterfly on its head has caused havoc in a few households. One, home where a 19 year old, Don Boggs, is under house arrest for drinking under age, the horse seemed to knock on the door and lead parents, Betty and Kent Boggs to a beer bottle hidden in their sons room. Yes, a horse! And what's going on with the weather in Westerly? A reporter has been sent to Westerly, in Latrain County. Stay tuned for further updates on this and other news. This is Joe Hart, Channel 95 news."

Now what? What are we going to do about this mess? Unfortunately, I had no time to think about this, there was another commotion coming from across the street.

The last time you read, Mr. Henry was taking Mrs. Henry, or the cat was taking the skunk into the house. Now, hours later, a grey van, driven by a skunk, was pulling into the Henry's garage, minus one mailbox, which was lying in the street. I swear, from my house, it looked like Mrs. Henry, or the skunk was on top of the cat, Mr. Henry!

C-RASH!

Instead of stopping before the garage wall, the van made a new entrance into the Henry household. Loud voices could be heard from the garage.

"AHHHHHHHhhhhh...!"

Running faster than a speeding car, and more quickly than Katie, or Katie in Lorraine Henry's body, I reached the Henry garage, with Ann fast approaching from behind.

"I told you to steer the car to the left." the cat yelled.

"I told you to hit the brake." the skunk yelled back.

"And, of course, we now need to find out if this is covered by the builder! What do I look up? Is a skunk driving a car, with a cat steering, covered?" Mr. Henry said waving with his paw.

The skunk raised her tail. We again moved not to get hit with her foul scent.

"Now, Lorraine, you have to control that temper of yours. You know what Dr. Z said, and that won't help us find Francois."

"Wait a minute," I interrupted. "Don't you think we should get into the house to discuss this? The hail is coming down pretty hard now and where is Francois?"

I continued.

"We were out putting up signs. Francois must have snuck out when Mr. Henry was airing out the house." the skunk replied. Her words were interrupted by the Katie. She tried to cover her nose with one hand and open the door with the other one. Francois was probably scared from all the things going on around her. Poor Francois!

"I will go look for Francois." Katie said. "Since I'm human or if that's what you call me, I won't draw attention." she continued.

"You're not funny!" shouted the skunk. "I'd like to...but I can't spray myself, could I?"

"She's trying to help us Lorrain, so don't be rude." Mr. Henry replied.

Katie disappeared out the door. We all spent the next few hours, just laughing and telling stories. Even, Mrs. Henry told some of her life experiences, too bad Katie wasn't there to enjoy!

The laughter was broke abruptly three hours after we entered the Henry home, when Katie entered followed by Francois, now back to her cat self. I looked in amazement as Mrs. Henry, whom was standing next to Katie, started changing right before my eyes! And Mr. Henry too!

I looked at my own body. Our bible verse from last week came into my mind, *"Be kind to one another, tender-hearted, forgiving each other, just as God in Christ also has forgiven you.´* Ephesians 4:32 (NIV) Bible. Amen!

"Ann!" I shouted as I lost my balance. The long legs and hoofs were now my own short human ones.

I stood there a moment, not believing my eyes. After a moment I was able to get my footing. I stumbled a few times. What do you expect; you would've done the same thing right? Now admit it.

A cheer rang through the house as each body transferred back to its original self.

"It looks like we might need some clothes!" squealed Katie as a few of us stood in our birthday suits or close to it.

"I will get a few blankets." said Mr. Henry, flashing a smile at his wife.

"Please hurry," Ann said with a moan. "Until then…" her words were cut off as she disappeared behind the couch. Everyone in the room ran to take cover. The only one still standing in her spot was Shadow. You know she didn't need any clothes, right? She had that beautiful coat of fur. Yes, we were all pretty much back to ourselves.

I wrapped the blanket Mr. Henry gave me around myself. I then cleared my throat and said, "Uh, it was fun being a deer, but I've learned that I do like being Jules Currier much better!"

And then, before anyone could comment, a commotion could be heard outside. Everyone wrapped in covers, ran to the window.

Wow! I thought. *I never saw so many people and cameras!*

The street was covered with people. And the people had cameras. Now, don't lie, were you one of those people? In a matter of seconds, it seemed like the crowd multiplied, until I couldn't see anything but people and cameras! And the rain, hail and lightning had stopped.

I spotted the local news anchors. The local radio broadcasters were interviewing the crowd.

Exodus 9:339(NIV) *"the thunder and hail stopped, and the rain no longer poured on the land,"* came into my mind. "**Thank you God**!" I said outload.

Behind me I heard Mrs. Henry clear throat. "There is clothing in the bathroom for all of you. I found some of our daughter, Grace's childhood clothing in an old box in the spare bedroom. Could you thank God for me also? What's so interesting outside?"

"GREG!" she shouted over the loud voices that carried into the house.

Suddenly, the Henry's doorbell rang. Yes, all of us were dressed or almost dressed in Grace Henry's clothes of twenty years ago.

Mrs. Henry looked at Mr. Henry and he nodded and quickly opened the door.

Chapter Seven
And What Happened in Westerly?

FLASH, FLASH, FLASH!

Hundreds of flashes, or it seemed like hundreds of flashes filled the Henry doorway. "Get those cameras out of my face," Mrs. Henry shouted over the videos cameras and flashing lights. "What do you think you're doing coming to my home and taking pictures without our permission?" she continued. "If you don't leave our property I will call our lawyer!"

"We were just checking to see if you've seen something unusual, Ma'am." Joe Hart, from Channel 95 News replied. "Have you even seen a skunk driving a car? How about a human in a tree mewing? And how about the rain, hail and lightning only in Westerly."

"Maybe in a cartoon, sir." the voice of Ed could be heard in the crowd. "Maybe you need to check into Knickerbockers Center. I'm sure they have a nice bed for you!"

And then, just before the police cars started coming down our street, the crowd moved toward Rose Court. Ed had already pushed himself through the crowd and was heading directly for the Henry door.

"Hey, Jules, it's nice to see my sister again." he said.

"Have you been hanging out in any duck ponds lately?" I asked.

"You betcha," he replied as he stepped into the Henry's house. "I taught those geese who's the omega!"

By the look on my face, everyone started laughing. Well, everyone but Ed. He shrugged. "Well, I did teach them a few things," he smiled. "And I bet you every duck in the pond will thank me!"

Suddenly, it seemed like we all recalled where we were and what just happened. By the look on Katie's face, I could tell she didn't know what to do. In fact, I didn't know what to do! Do you? It was pretty quiet for a few minutes. It seemed like everyone was holding their breath, or maybe I thought so because I was.

Mrs. Henry cleared her voice and with one hand on Katie's shoulder, she motioned towards the dining room, "Please, join Greg and me for some cake and a glass of milk."

Katie looked at me and back at Mrs. Henry. "Sure, a piece of cake would be nice.'

Now, there you have it. That's what happened in my city, Westerly, Ohio. I bet you want to come visit us, right? Well, we would love to see you? The only thing is, well, I know, or I believe I know what happened that Friday. Anyway, well Ann won't talk about that day. Okay, fine, if she wants to make believe it didn't happen, go figure! The point is do you believe it happened? No lying.

And of course, there are more important issues

besides my dear friend, Ann. I learned a few things that day. I now KNOW that God looks after us. He looked after me that day and the many days that followed. I now don't or try not to let people like Brenda Appletree bother me. I'd be lying if I said it's easy. Of course nothing is easy, unless it's writing for the school newspaper. Did I tell you I was accepted on our Junior High newspaper staff? Yes, I Jules Currier am now in Junior High now.

Anyway, Ann is still taking woodworking classes. She's made a few tables and carved a nice eagle that is on the wall in the Ostrander family room.

Ed, he's still hanging out at the duck pond. No joke, he got a job cleaning the pond. I guess before that day, they couldn't keep help. The blond mallard wouldn't let anyone near the pond.

Pastor Allen has retired, but his stories will always make me smile. I heard the Allen's have opened a gift store in southern, Ohio. Pastor Linch is also gone. She now preaches in a church in another county. I'll always think of her when I see a butterfly. My family and Ann's now serve in another church in Latrain County. Yes, we serve in the Children's Ministry.

Shadow, well she's still shy, but she seems to like

the Mayor, go figure! And the Mayor, well, that following Monday, he agreed to allow the girl scouts to use vacant land for the first 'Puppy Park,' in our area. I even heard that the Mayor himself donated not just his time, but money for the project! Please check it out when you come visit us.

Of course, I'm still waiting for you to knock on my door. So, what's keeping you? Now, you aren't worried that you might turn into a skunk, cat, eagle, blond mallard, Mayor, deer or something, do you?

I bet you're wondering about Katie, Mrs. Henry and Mr. Henry? Well, I can't speak for them, but there was definitely a change in their lives! I can see Mrs. Henry hide a smile when Katie is on her knees cleaning the driveway. Hey, what did you expect? It's nice to know that some things never change.

Mrs. Henry opened a dance studio near the high school. I heard Katie just might take a class. Go figure. She didn't even want to learn or like to dance before that weekend! And the Henry's might volunteer at the 'Puppy Park."

Of course, the news people played the story of a dog playing golf and a skunk driving a car as far as they could. Now they shrugged the story off for new news like, we did get a new President. And it's alright to eat chocolate, or is it now? I just wish they'd make up their minds, don't you?

Then there's Wave and Michael Kordic. I heard Mr. Kordic is still playing golf. Did you hear they are 'Couple of the year,' this year? They will be a sweet 'Corn Couple,' don't you think?

And our development, well there's a few hills left to hang out. We have a few new streets since I starting writing this story. We now hang out at each other's homes instead of hills.

And finally, there's Westerly. It's still the festival capital of the Latrain County. And with the new 'Puppy Park,' Wag-Your-Tail Barkery has so much business that Wave Kordic might have to add on or build somewhere else in the city. I still can't tell why our city loves corn so much, but who doesn't? But I'll still try to find out before you visit or better yet, that will be your job to find out, ok?

I almost forgot to tell you the big news! There is a new ride at the Popcorn Festival. It's called the 'Skunk Ride.' And that ride's VERY popular with the tourists! You must check it out.

Now that I've recapped how everyone is in Westerly, I must get ready for my new story. I just received a text message from the editor of my junior high newspaper. The text read: **"Breaking News: Someone or something is leaving unwanted surprises outside the Appletree house. The Appletree's are on night patrol to find the culprit and bring the person or thing to justice. Jules, please report on this immediately! They say a blond mallard has been seen outside the Appletree residence."**

No, sorry everyone, it wasn't me! I may not like them, but...hey, you tried to get the scoop! A journalist isn't allowed to give away the facts to a case, so don't try to get any more details from me. I know this one will make the news! So, I guess there will be one less person at our dinner table tonight! I've got to run. See you when the next edition comes out.

It's carnival time! Will Jules Currier and her friends survive the morning's mishaps, or will trouble prevent the young friends from going to the carnival? What happens when the children face adventure, dread, confusion, and faith all in 24 hours? Will chaos win? You, the reader can search for clues throughout the story to see why circumstances happen when wrong decisions are made. Find that each and every one of us is unique and human. Adults even Pastors, eat, sleep and yes, even use the bathroom.

Once mistakes are made, the reader finds they can be made right. An enemy can become a friend. God loves everyone, even naughty children!

A fun read for children and adult alike.

Made in the USA
Lexington, KY
15 April 2017